SCOOBY-DOO!™
BATTLE OF THE SNOWBOARDERS

Written by Sonia Sander
Illustrated by Alcadia SNC

WITHDRAWN

WB

ABDO
Spotlight

ABDOPUBLISHING.COM

Reinforced library bound edition published in 2016 by Spotlight, a division of ABDO
PO Box 398166, Minneapolis, Minnesota 55439. Spotlight produces high-quality
reinforced library bound editions for schools and libraries. Published by agreement
with Warner Bros. Entertainment Inc.

Printed in the United States of America, North Mankato, Minnesota.
092015
012016

THIS BOOK CONTAINS
RECYCLED MATERIALS

CATALOGING-IN-PUBLICATION DATA

Sander, Sonia.
 Scooby-Doo and the battle of the snowboarders / Sonia Sander.
  p. cm. (Scooby-Doo leveled readers)
 Summary: A scary snow monster is sabotaging the big race. Can Mystery, Inc. find the monster
and save the snowboarders?
 1. Scooby-Doo (Fictitious character)--Juvenile fiction. 2. Dogs--Juvenile fiction. 3. Mystery and
detective stories--Juvenile fiction. 4. Adventure and adventures--Juvenile fiction.
 [Fic]--dc23
         2015156076

 978-1-61479-415-8   (Reinforced Library Bound Edition)

Spotlight

A Division of ABDO
abdopublishing.com

It was time for the VonWinter snowboard contest.

The gang arrived at the lodge a few days early.

Scooby wanted to try the course before the big race.

Scooby said hello to Victor VonWinter, the owner of the resort.

The year before, his nephew Chase just beat out Scooby for the trophy.

"Better luck this year," said Victor VonWinter.

"When a VonWinter is in the race, no one else has a chance," said Chase.

"Like, that was a sticky shake Chase gave us," said Shaggy as they walked away.

"Rasty, roo," said Scooby, licking marshmallow off his paw.

Out on the course, Shaggy and Scooby were warned about slippery and sticky rails and pipes. There was even talk of a glowing monster.

Scooby had been training all year.

"Like, I don't care what Chase says, Scoob," said Shaggy. "You're the one to beat!"

Scooby was in top form until he hit the first rail.

Then he was flying out of control.

"Like, maybe make that move simpler, Scoob," said Shaggy.

The next rail slowed Scooby right down.
He couldn't move at all.
Scooby was stuck in a marshmallow goo!
"Like, that's a little too simple, Scoob,"
said Shaggy.

Scooby was in trouble.

Shaggy rushed over to help.

But suddenly, a glowing monster appeared at the top of the hill.

One look at the monster and Scooby jumped out of his snowboard as fast as he could and ran.

Shaggy and Scooby raced across the snow. They finally lost the glowing monster when they fell into a hidden hole in the snow.

"Like, maybe those rumors about the monster were true," said Shaggy.

Fred, Daphne and Velma saw the whole chase from the lodge.

They arrived just in time to dig Shaggy and Scooby out.

"T-t-t-h-h-h-a-a-a-n-n-n-k-k-s!" said Shaggy, shaking.

"Like, aren't the northern lights meant to be pretty not creepy?" asked Shaggy.

"Like, there's always next year, Scoob!" said Shaggy.

"Scooby didn't train all year to quit now," said Fred.

"Come on, let's find out what's really going on here."

The gang looked for clues all over the lodge. The last place they went was the kitchen.

"Like, the only clues I want to see are cookie crumbs," said Shaggy.

"Jeepers!" cried Daphne. "That's one slippery floor."

"It's olive oil from those empty cans," said Fred.

Shaggy and Scooby continued hunting for food.

But they found more than a snack.

Just then the monster burst into the room.

"Zoinks! Run!" cried Shaggy. "It's that glowing creep again!"

"Quick!" cried Fred. "Hide in the pantry!"

"This place is sure well-lit for a pantry," said Daphne, pointing up to a row of very bright lights.

"Jinkies," said Velma. "There's also a lot of marshmallows for so little hot chocolate."

"Like, Scoob and I can help fix that," said Shaggy as he tossed Scooby a marshmallow.

"We have to stop this monster before it ruins the race," said Fred.

"We'll need a pretty strong plan to stop him," said Daphne.

"There's nothing stronger than a snowstorm," said Fred.

"And I think I know where we can get a blizzard."

Victor VonWinter was more than happy to lend his snow machines to the gang.

After setting the machines to blizzard, the gang put part two of their plan to work.

Scooby took a few runs down the course to lure out the monster.

It wasn't long before a spooky glow could be seen on Scooby's heels.

As soon as Scooby flew across the finish line, the gang was ready to trap the glowing monster.

It was buried in a huge pile of snow in no time.

Velma unmasked the monster. It was Chase VonWinter!

"The marshmallow on your hands gave you away, Chase," said Velma.

"I couldn't risk losing the race and my family's honor," said Chase.

"I would have won, too, if it weren't for you meddling kids."

"Our family doesn't have to cheat to win," Victor said to Chase.
"Take him away officers!"

"I can't thank you enough for saving the race," said Victor.

"As a show of gratitude, all your meals are free."

"Like, show me the way to the dining room," said Shaggy.

"Ruh-huh," said Scooby, nodding his head.

With Chase the cheater gone, the race was monster-free. Scooby easily won the trophy. Scooby-Dooby-Doo!